MUSIC USE NOTE

Licensees are solely responsible for obtaining formal written permission from copyright owners to use copyrighted music in the performance of this play and are strongly cautioned to do so. If no such permission is obtained by the licensee, then the licensee must use only original music that the licensee owns and controls. Licensees are solely responsible and liable for all music clearances and shall indemnify the copyright owners of the play(s) and their licensing agent, Samuel French, against any costs, expenses, losses and liabilities arising from the use of music by licensees. Please contact the appropriate music licensing authority in your territory for the rights to any incidental music.

IMPORTANT BILLING AND CREDIT REQUIREMENTS

If you have obtained performance rights to this title, please refer to your licensing agreement for important billing and credit requirements.

LIZARDS... was originally produced at the University of Minnesota's Guthrie Theatre on April 11, 2007. The production was Directed by Josh Hecht with the following cast:

VICTOR	Ricardo Vázquez
JESSE	John Kelley
PHOEBE	Valeri Mudek
RONNIE	Amanda Fuller
SEBASTIAN	Jake Ford
MALLORY	Caroline Cooney

Set Designer	Joseph Stanley
Costume Designer	Juli Acton
Lighting Designer	Ray Steveson
Sound Designer	Mike Hallenbeck
Dramaturg	Carla Steen
Voice and Speech Consultants	Elisa Carlson, Lucinda Holshue
Movement Consultant	Randy Reyes
Stage Manager	Adam Ehret
Assistant Stage Managers	Sharon Bach, Sara Swanberg

Maggie Lombard
760 814 4698
152 lines

Lizards...

Megan Mostyn-Brown

Breakfast scene: Sweats, barefeet, & crop top

Park: ~~Jeans~~ leggings, whole foods, hat, sneakers, jean jacket

Storeroom: ↑

Night: ↑, but barefoot

A SAMUEL FRENCH ACTING EDITION

SAMUEL FRENCH
FOUNDED 1830

SAMUELFRENCH.COM
SAMUELFRENCH-LONDON.CO.UK

Copyright © 2011 by Megan Mostyn-Brown
All Rights Reserved

LIZARDS... is fully protected under the copyright laws of the United States of America, the British Commonwealth, including Canada, and all other countries of the Copyright Union. All rights, including professional and amateur stage productions, recitation, lecturing, public reading, motion picture, radio broadcasting, television and the rights of translation into foreign languages are strictly reserved.

ISBN 978-0-573-65113-7

www.SamuelFrench.com
www.SamuelFrench-London.co.uk

For Production Enquiries

United States and Canada
Info@SamuelFrench.com
1-866-598-8449

United Kingdom and Europe
Plays@SamuelFrench-London.co.uk
020-7255-4302

Each title is subject to availability from Samuel French, depending upon country of performance. Please be aware that *LIZARDS...* may not be licensed by Samuel French in your territory. Professional and amateur producers should contact the nearest Samuel French office or licensing partner to verify availability.

CAUTION: Professional and amateur producers are hereby warned that *LIZARDS...* is subject to a licensing fee. Publication of this play(s) does not imply availability for performance. Both amateurs and professionals considering a production are strongly advised to apply to Samuel French before starting rehearsals, advertising, or booking a theatre. A licensing fee must be paid whether the title(s) is presented for charity or gain and whether or not admission is charged. Professional/Stock licensing fees are quoted upon application to Samuel French.

No one shall make any changes in this title(s) for the purpose of production. No part of this book may be reproduced, stored in a retrieval system, or transmitted in any form, by any means, now known or yet to be invented, including mechanical, electronic, photocopying, recording, videotaping, or otherwise, without the prior written permission of the publisher. No one shall upload this title(s), or part of this title(s), to any social media websites.

For all enquiries regarding motion picture, television, and other media rights, please contact Samuel French.

CHARACTERS

PHOEBE – 23, married, Valium addict, lost
JESSE – 23, Phoebe's husband, passive aggressive, a fixer
MALLORY – 26, shy, nervous, making a big change
SEBASTIAN – 25, laid back, pothead, thinks he's a loser
RONNIE – 25, Punk, sassy, former Jersey girl, in love with Sebastian
VICTOR – 28, nervous, sweet, making a big change

SETTING

Various locations in New York City and the Bronx

SCENE 1

(The play takes place in various places around New York during the end of September over the course of one day. The set should just suggest where they are. Like a bench or two chairs or whatever.

The Bronx. In black, rowdy classroom sounds. Spotlight up on VICTOR, 20s he wears a short sleeved button down, pants and loosened tie. He is sweating profusely and looks harried. A blackboard is behind him. He writes down various words during the lesson.)

VICTOR. Okay...okay settle down... I said settle down... yes Shanikwa I know it is hot I opened the windows that's the best I can do... now everyone take out your notebooks and a pencil... Daytwon put away your markers and take out a pencil... a pencil Daytwon not a pen... thank you... now today we are going to continue our lesson on lizards... Yesterday we learned that lizards are what? Anyone? Anyone?

(Lights up downstage on PHOEBE in an apartment in Brooklyn. She sits at a table staring at two pills in front of her.)

VICTOR. Well at least now you're quiet... Lizards are reptiles... There are many different species of lizards... I don't see anyone writing... you should be writing down the word species... I have a feeling it may be on your spelling test on Monday... species means type... one type of lizard is the- Faruk! FARUK! Ashlan wake Faruk up... thank you... Good morning Faruk thank you for joining our class we are taking notes on lizards... one species of lizard is the glass lizard... glass lizards have legs they can't use and actually look more like snakes than our class gecko... but like their other lizard friends their tails do break off as a defense mechanism...

(JESSE enters behind PHOEBE. He stops and stares at her from behind. She doesn't notice him.)

VICTOR. Now many lizards change color in response to their environments- No Alizé you may not go to the bathroom you went ten minutes ago- As I was saying many lizards change color as a response to their environment or in response to stress... the most common lizard that changes color is the? Anyone?

(PHOEBE crushes the pills with the spoon. JESSE doesn't move.)

VICTOR. Yes that's right Fredrick...the chameleon...why aren't you writing Maya? Borrow paper from your neighbor and tell your grandmother you need a notebook for science, now as we learned yesterday lizards eat rodents or insects and therefore are harmless to humans...

(PHOEBE snorts the powder off the table.)

VICTOR. Yes Stasia the Komodo dragon may attack people but there are none of them in the Bronx so you have nothing to worry about...now where was I? I don't remember and we only have five minutes left so I'll leave you with this lizards regenerate...meaning if their leg or their tail is cut off that means it can grow back- Daytwon that information does not give you license to karate chop Bernards leg- okay everyone just settle down... Uggh...just...just draw in your notebooks until the music teacher arrives or something...Fredrick bring me Jimmy...no Jimmy the gecko...it's time to feed him...he's not what? He's not moving?

(VICTOR sighs as lights go down on him. JESSE moves towards PHOEBE.)

JESSE. That's not much of a breakfast.
PHOEBE. Shit! You scared me.
JESSE. Sorry.
PHOEBE. You shouldn't sneak up on people like that.
JESSE. You shouldn't be doing shit that people need to sneak up on.

(Lights up across the stage on RONNIE and SEBASTIAN in another apartment in Brooklyn. They are sitting on beanbag chairs playing Play Station.)

PHOEBE. I'm an adult I can do whatever I want. [handwritten: mocking]

JESSE. Okaaay...But I don't think when the doctor prescribed those to you he intended you to snort them.

PHOEBE. Were you in the doctor's office when he prescribed them? [handwritten: ??? Hmmm?]

JESSE. No.

PHOEBE. I didn't think so.

(Beat.)

JESSE. Have you heard back about any of those museum jobs?

PHOEBE. No I've been too- Jesus- Have you worked on your big novel?

JESSE. No I've been working at a shit job to support us.

PHOEBE. Don't do that.

JESSE. What?

PHOEBE. Blame me.

JESSE. I'm not-

PHOEBE. I'm trying. It's juss with everything that's- juss gimme a fucking break okay.

JESSE. Phebes why won't you talk to me about this?

PHOEBE. Cuz I've got nothing to say.

JESSE. I find that hard to believe.

PHOEBE. Well its true.

JESSE. Phoebe it's been three months.

PHOEBE. I drowned Jesse.

JESSE. You almost drowned. If you had drowned you'd be dead.

PHOEBE. That's insensitive.

JESSE. Sorry, I'm sorry-I'm just trying to put things in perspective.

PHOEBE. Well I guess our perspectives don't see eye to eye.

JESSE. Well maybe they could if you just opened up to me.

PHOEBE. Like I said I've got nothing to say to you.

JESSE. Ummm... did I do something I wasn't aware of?

(She doesn't answer. Maybe she rubs her eyes or her temple or something.)

JESSE. Cuz as far as I know I have been trying to be supportive of all of this... giving you space and time when you needed it... allowing you to work this out on your own because you don't seem to want to talk to me... so if there's something I did or didn't do that will make this all better just tell me and I'll do it.

(Beat.)

JESSE. Look I ahhh I can take off work tomorrow. So I can go with you to swimming lessons.
PHOEBE. You don't have to.
JESSE. I want to.
PHOEBE. I want to go by myself.
JESSE. Well I thought you might need some-
PHOEBE. You don't always have to be there for everything okay?
JESSE. I'm sorry- I just...never mind.
PHOEBE. You know maybe you should try doing something for yourself by yourself sometime.
JESSE. *(Mumbling.)* Maybe I'll pick up a heroin addiction.
PHOEBE. What?
JESSE. Nothing.
PHOEBE. Juss go tah work Jesse. You're gonna be late.

(Beat.)

JESSE. I'll umm be home around seven.

(JESSE goes to kiss PHOEBE but then decides against it. He exits. PHOEBE doesn't watch him leave. RONNIE and SEBASTIAN play intently.)

SEBASTIAN. Fuck!

(Lights out on PHOEBE.)

RONNIE. Ha-ha sucker. Once again I have the high ranking score. So kiss it!

SEBASTIAN. Yeah, yeah, yeah... It was luck...

RONNIE. Fuck luck! I have beaten you twelve times in a row...

SEBASTIAN. Like I said...

(RONNIE punches him in the shoulder. He punches her back.)

RONNIE. Will the illustrious Sheryl be here when I get back?

SEBASTIAN. Nope. We broke up.

RONNIE. Broke up?

SEBASTIAN. Did I stutter?

RONNIE. No I'm just shocked. You guys... seemed so... I mean you were really into her...

SEBASTIAN. Guess she wasn't as in to me...

RONNIE. Fabulous. I can actually sleep in the apartment where I pay half the rent?

SEBASTIAN. Don't play like that. Once, once I asked you to sleep at Victor's. And it was on our anniversary.

RONNIE. Sure... whatever... ding dong the bitch is dead that's all I have to say...

SEBASTIAN. Thanks for the love in my time of need...

(Lights up on MALLORY. She is in a travel agency in Brooklyn. She sits in a chair fidgeting nervously, clutching her purse.)

RONNIE. She's a wannabe actress who works at Prada...yer a jobless hippie who majored in Philosophy...I could gladly see the end of that relationship a mile away.

(MALLORY puts down her bag and then changes her mind and puts it back in her lap.)

SEBASTIAN. God yer a bitch sometimes...

RONNIE. I try... you know there's a message on the machine from Phebes.

SEBASTIAN. Yeah I got it...

RONNIE. You guys have been spending a lot of time together...

SEBASTIAN. She's still a little fucked up...

RONNIE. It's been months.

SEBASTIAN. She needs someone to talk to.

RONNIE. Well she hasn't been talking to me about it.

SEBASTIAN. What are you trying to say?

RONNIE. Me n' Phoebe are close. It's juss ya know odd er whatever...

SEBASTIAN. Look I dunno why she's talking to me and not you. She just is.

RONNIE. Her own personal hero.

SEBASTIAN. What the fuck is that supposed to mean?

RONNIE. Nothing... you guys just didn't really get along all that well before... and now... maybe Sheryl was jealous of your new friend...

SEBASTIAN. First of all Phoebe is your friend... and as I've said before she feels like she owes me for what happened at the beach... and secondly Sheryl dumped me because she met someone else...

RONNIE. Well does Jesse know you guys are "hangin' out"?

(Beat.)

SEBASTIAN. I dunno. That's her business.

RONNIE. I mean he's her husband.

SEBASTIAN. Look we're just hanging out - talking or whatever - you're making it into some big fucking mystery that it's not... so quit tryin' to invent shit that's not there drama empress.

RONNIE. I was just pushing your buttons Mr. Sensitive... if your gonna dish it out learn to take it... Jesus...

SEBASTIAN. Whatever...

(Beat.)

RONNIE. On that note the world of overpriced groceries calls me...

(SEBASTIAN starts a new game and ignores her. RONNIE stands staring at him. MALLORY puts her purse back on the ground.)

RONNIE. Peace out.

(She lingers for a second. JESSE enters and sits at his desk across from MALLORY. Lights out on RONNIE and SEBASTIAN. MALLORY picks up her purse again.)

JESSE. Hello Ms. Daniels. I'm Jesse.
MALLORY. Hey. And it's Mallory. Ms. Daniels makes me feel like I'm old.
JESSE. No problem. Mallory. So where can I book you a trip today?
MALLORY. I'm thinking of... I'm thinking of taking a trip to ummm Brazil...
JESSE. Brazil... okay...
MALLORY. You ever been there?
JESSE. I haven't traveled much.
MALLORY. Oh.
JESSE. But I've heard Rio is a blast.

(Beat.)

JESSE. So how long are you looking to go for?
MALLORY. A travel agent who doesn't travel... that's kind of ironic...
JESSE. Interim job...this is I mean... my wife and I are in a little debt... maybe we'll be able to travel at some point...
MALLORY. Oh.
JESSE. Anyway how long you looking to go for?
MALLORY. I'm not sure... maybe just a one way ticket.
JESSE. I wouldn't suggest a one way ticket... you'll get a better deal if you book round trip...
MALLORY. I don't know if I want to come back...
JESSE. It's only a few hundred dollars to change your return ticket. It'll cost you a lot more to book a one way return ticket from down there if you decide to leave.
MALLORY. Oh... okay...
JESSE. So round trip... to Rio?
MALLORY. How long have you been married?
JESSE. Huh?
MALLORY. You look to young to be married.

JESSE. You look to young to be fleeing the country...

MALLORY. I'm not fleeing... I'm.... vacationing I guess... ummm

JESSE. We've been married for a year. But we've been together since tenth grade.

MALLORY. Wow...

JESSE. Yep...

MALLORY. You must be really happy together...

JESSE. Yeah... yeah we are... Phoebe... my wife... she's great... more importantly though... your trip...

MALLORY. I'd like to leave as soon as possible...

JESSE. Like how soon?

MALLORY. End of the week if I can...

JESSE. You know there's a lot of paperwork on your end involved in something like this.

MALLORY. I have a passport. I've researched the rest of the paperwork it should be no problem getting it done.

JESSE. And you still claim you're not fleeing?

(Beat. Lights up on PHOEBE and RONNIE. They are on a bench in Union Square. They wear Whole Foods T-shirts. RONNIE eats a sandwich. PHOEBE pushes food around in a plastic container.)

JESSE. Yer not the first one. Most people book trips to Canada or Sweden, though. Sick of New York, sick of the government, trying to see if there's any place freer in the Free World.

MALLORY. I'm making a change. If I don't commit to it now I'm afraid I'll back out.

JESSE. Flying to a country you've never been to and don't know anyone might be something you want to think over.

(Beat.)

MALLORY. Book me a one way ticket to Rio as soon as possible.

JESSE. You sure?

MALLORY. Yeah.

(Lights out on MALLORY and JESSE.)

BIRTHDAY 15

RONNIE. I'm gonna turn into a piece of fucking alfalfa one of these days... *Munchin on bread*

(PHOEBE doesn't respond.)

RONNIE. Earth to Phebes...I was being humorous if you didn't notice...
PHOEBE. Sorry...
RONNIE. Okay so maybe my big news will shock you into being present in the world.
PHOEBE. Go for it.
RONNIE. Sheryl dumped Sebastian.
PHOEBE. Hm...
RONNIE. Hm?! I have been waiting for them to break up for six months now and all you can fucking say is "hm"?
PHOEBE. Sorry I'm a little out of it...
RONNIE. Maybe if you ate your food instead of pushing it around...
PHOEBE. I ate a big breakfast.
RONNIE. A big breakfast of what?
PHOEBE. Do you think Andy has anything on him today?
RONNIE. Didn't you just buy a stash from him the other day?
PHOEBE. I'm out.

(Beat.)

RONNIE. How long have we known each other?
PHOEBE. Ummm... I dunno since I moved here. Like a year and a half.
RONNIE. Well then I'm gonna refrain from commenting on the fact that you've recently become a shade of your former self.
PHOEBE. Wasn't that just a comment?
RONNIE. Not in my book.
PHOEBE. Whatever...
RONNIE. Don't be a fucking statistic.
PHOEBE. I thought you weren't going to comment.
RONNIE. I changed my mind.
PHOEBE. I'd appreciate it if you changed it back.
RONNIE. Too late. You're turning into a cliche Phoebe.

PHOEBE. Spare me the lecture Ronnie.

RONNIE. It's not a lecture. It's an observation. You've become an overeducated pill-popping housewife.

PHOEBE. I'm not a housewife. I have a job.

RONNIE. At a glorified grocery store.

PHOEBE. Did you not notice the green Whole Foods shirt on your back? Or the fact that you've been scanning soy products for the last four hours.

RONNIE. Yes but I don't have a fancy pants art history degree. In fact I don't have a degree at all. And for the record, nobody expected anything more from me than managing the Sunglass Hut at the Short Hills Mall. So really my situation is a big step up for my lack of education and trashy Jersey background.

PHOEBE. Way to be motivated Ronnie.

RONNIE. My point is you've been eating downers like Skittles.

PHOEBE. You sound like Jesse.

RONNIE. Maybe Jesse isn't so wrong.

PHOEBE. Fuck off, okay?

RONNIE. I'm juss sayin'-

PHOEBE. I don't need you siding with him.

RONNIE. If it walks like a duck and talks like a duck-

PHOEBE. I've been having flashbacks. The pills help. Now does Andy have anything on him?

RONNIE. Last time I checked my name was not Andy.

(Beat.)

PHOEBE. I'm sorry... for... snapping...
RONNIE. No problem.

(Beat.)

RONNIE. You hanging out with Sebastian later?
PHOEBE. Maybe.
RONNIE. Hmmm... I find it all very interesting..
PHOEBE. Are you jealous?
RONNIE. No!
PHOEBE. Cuz you sound like yer jealous.
RONNIE. I am not jealous... of you... yer married...

PHOEBE. You have nothing to worry about... there's nothing going on... I just feel- it just helps to talk to him about it.
RONNIE. Totally understandable.

(Beat.)

RONNIE. So what are you guys gonna do when you hang out?
PHOEBE. Really fun secret things that don't involve you.
RONNIE. Yer so fucking funny.
PHOEBE. I try my best.

(RONNIE rolls her eyes.)

RONNIE. I'm gonna head back in.
PHOEBE I'll meet you in a minute.

(Beat. RONNIE gets up.)

PHOEBE. Are you goinna to tell him you love him?
RONNIE. Huh?
PHOEBE. Sebastian. Now that he's free. Are you goinna to tell him you're in love with him?

(Beat. RONNIE shrugs.)

RONNIE. Andy's working in the bakery. I think he breaks at two.

(RONNIE exits. A beat. Lights up on the other side of the park. VICTOR sits on another bench. MALLORY enters and sits on the other end of the bench. Lights out on PHOEBE. VICTOR drinks a beer hidden in a paper bag. MALLORY begins to take out a series of small Tupperware containers. They contain her lunch.)

VICTOR. You really like Tupperware.

(MALLORY checks him out and quickly begins putting her food back in her bag.)

VICTOR. No, no don't leave...I'm not some crazy drunk. I'm a fourth grade teacher.
MALLORY. Most fourth grade teachers don't ummm...do that at lunch.
VICTOR. Well as of an hour ago I'm not one anymore.
MALLORY. Oh I'm sorry...

(MALLORY goes to leave again.)

VICTOR. Don't go... You're very pretty... I just walked out on my job... my day would be a whole lot better if I could just sit on a bench and chat with a pretty girl.

(MALLORY stares at him.)

VICTOR. I'm twenty-eight. I was a teaching fellow. I own a cat named Snuggles. Really, I'm harmless.

(MALLORY sits back down.)

VICTOR. Sorry, I'm a little...It's been a long day.
MALLORY. You think I'm pretty?
VICTOR. Yeah, yeah...I like your glasses. You've got that sexy librarian thing going on.

(MALLORY angrily stands back up.)

VICTOR. No, no I didn't mean it in a derogatory way. I meant it in the best possible non-threatening sort of fashion. Just sit back down. Please.

(MALLORY tentatively sits back down.)

VICTOR. I'm Victor Aufthausen.
MALLORY. Oh...ummm I'm Mallory Daniels.

(Beat.)

MALLORY. You're German?
VICTOR. Puerto Rican. I'm adopted. My adopted parents are German. Well German-American I guess. Whatever...

MALLORY. I don't know what I am.

VICTOR. I'd say you're definitely not Puerto Rican.

MALLORY. Yeah well- I meant I guess I'm a mutt. One of those Anglo Saxon European sort of mutts.

VICTOR. It suits you well.

MALLORY. Really?

VICTOR. I find your features rather calming. You could be a chameleon in any situation with your ambiguous European palate.

MALLORY. More like a wallflower actually.

VICTOR. Same difference depending on the situation.

MALLORY. You're weird.

VICTOR. Funny... my students often said the same thing.

MALLORY. That ummm... why you quit?

VICTOR. You ever taught a class of thirty-six fourth graders?

MALLORY. No.

VICTOR They're loud...and rowdy... and there's too may of them... which isn't their fault it's the school system's... and a lot of them have parents who don't care... or do care but don't have the money to pay for school supplies or don't speak English so can't read the school supplies list... I've spent over two hundred dollars this year of my own money on crayons and pens and paper and pencils... and we've only been in school for a few weeks... which that doesn't even compare to the hundreds of dollars I spent on shit like that last year...

MALLORY. Wow...

VICTOR. Yeah... and I bought a gecko for the class... a class pet of sorts cuz we're learning about lizards...and it died... it died because the kids were so excited to have an animal in class... most of them haven't ever had a pet... that they kept touching it and touching it... three and four and five of them at a time screaming and touching even though I told them not too...and I know they were just excited... but we had a rule in class...two at a time... be quiet or you'll scare it to death... I think he had a heart attack from all the attention...

MALLORY. So you left?

VICTOR. You know that song- Jesus I can't remember the title- anyway it's the one where they say "I am the walrus"?

MALLORY. Sure...

VICTOR. I kept hearing "I am the gecko" in my head over and over again in the tune of that song and I figured it wasn't a good thing.
MALLORY. Wow...
VICTOR. Yeah... So I walked out after science buried the gecko in an empty lot near the school and then took the train down here...

(MALLORY stares at him.)

VICTOR. Could you please stop looking at me like I'm crazy?
MALLORY. I'm not... I just...
VICTOR. I shared too much didn't I?
MALLORY. No, no.
VICTOR. It's been a long day.
MALLORY. I can tell.
VICTOR. Your day? How has your day been?
MALLORY. Oh... ummm... I ahhh... I booked a trip.
VICTOR. Really? Where?
MALLORY. Brazil. I'm going to Brazil.
VICTOR. So I was right.
MALLORY. About what?
VICTOR. You're not the wallflower you claim to be.

(MALLORY blushes.)

MALLORY. Looking for a change...
VICTOR. Today seems to be the day to do that.
MALLORY. Mhmm...yeah I guess...

(Pause.)

VICTOR. Would you like to have a drink some time?
MALLORY. With you?
VICTOR. No with that guy over there in the bicycle shorts.

(MALLORY stares at him.)

VICTOR. Sorry I was making a joke. A bad joke at that. Of course I meant with me.

MALLORY. I booked a trip, though.
VICTOR. People who vacation can still go on dates.
MALLORY. No I'm leaving in a week.
VICTOR. Oh... that sucks.
MALLORY. Sorry.
VICTOR. Brazil is a lucky place.
MALLORY. What?
VICTOR. To have you. You're nice and a good listener. This city doesn't have many good listeners. And you're pretty to boot.

(Beat. She closes her eyes and reopens them.)

MALLORY. Woah...
VICTOR. What?
MALLORY. I just... I got umm a little woozy for a second.
VICTOR. You sure you're okay?
MALLORY. Yeah, you know I guess umm... I guess I could go for a drink tonight.
VICTOR. Really?
MALLORY. Yeah, yeah. Why not?
VICTOR. Okay... um there's a bar on Perry Street called the Other Room. It's quiet on Wednesday nights. Maybe around nine tonight.
MALLORY. Sure.

(Lights out on the bench. Lights up on PHOEBE in her Whole Foods uniform. She sits on a chair in a dimly lit area of what could be the stock room. A few boxes are stacked behind her. She hums as she pulls all but 2 pills out of a plastic bag and shoves them in her pocket. The two remaining pills she crushes in the bag with her foot and then carefully turns the baggie inside out to snort the powder. As she snorts SEBASTIAN walks in.)

SEBASTIAN. Hey.

(PHOEBE quickly wipes her nose.)

PHOEBE. Hey.
SEBASTIAN. No need to front. I've been standing in the doorway watching you.

PHOEBE. You must be taking tips from Jesse.
SEBASTIAN. Huh?
PHOEBE. He snuck up on me this morning.
SEBASTIAN. Oh.

(Beat.)

PHOEBE. Thanks fer meeting me.
SEBASTIAN. No problem.

(Beat.)

SEBASTIAN. You okay?
PHOEBE. I dunno. Ummm... you can sit down if you want.

(He sits. Beat.)

SEBASTIAN. So...
PHOEBE. So?
SEBASTIAN. Ronnie working? I didn't see her when I came through.
PHOEBE. Yeah she's in the deli.

(Beat.)

SEBASTIAN. So... what's up?
PHOEBE. I'm sitting in the back room of a Whole Foods and in about five minutes I'll be stoned.
SEBASTIAN. Cool... so then why'd you call me?
PHOEBE. Cuz you don't have a job so you can come by and hang out in the afternoon.
SEBASTIAN. Yeah, yeah...okay "Ronnie"...
PHOEBE. Sorry... truth is I'm off work and I don't feel like going home... Or being alone.
SEBASTIAN. You know, up until a few months ago you thought I was an asshole.
PHOEBE. Shit changes.
SEBASTIAN. Okay cool...
PHOEBE. You're free to leave at anytime...

(Pause. She stares at him.)

(Beat.)

PHOEBE. *(As if realizing it for the first time.)* But he didn't jump in.
SEBASTIAN. Who?
PHOEBE. Jesse. He grabbed me after. But he didn't jump in when I was drowning.
SEBASTIAN. Phoebe don't fuckin' go down that road-
PHOEBE. He should've gotten to me first.
SEBASTIAN. What happened, happened.
PHOEBE. We've been together since tenth grade-
SEBASTIAN. You can't blame him-
PHOEBE. You're the one who saved me-
SEBASTIAN. Phoebe...
PHOEBE. No. The point of all of this is Jesse didn't. You did. You didn't even like me that much and you saved me.

(Beat. He looks at her. She kisses him. He is caught off guard at first and then kisses her back for a second before pulling away and:)

SEBASTIAN. Woah, okay woah, we can't...
PHOEBE. But I thought-
SEBASTIAN. Just forget what you thought...
PHOEBE. But you kissed me back-
SEBASTIAN. It was a mistake. Yer married-
PHOEBE. But-
SEBASTIAN. Yer married.
PHOEBE. I know but-
SEBASTIAN. Look Phoebe I am glad that I can be here to help you as a friend- and yes I'll fuckin' admit I like this hanging out thing with you cuz strangely you've become one ah the only people in my life who being around doesn't make me feel like a loser douchebag but- fuck- you can't be making all of this out to mean more than it does...
PHOEBE. I almost died and you saved me.
SEBASTIAN. True but I ahh I don't think that means we should make out.
PHOEBE. But you're the only person who really seems to understand what I'm- where I'm-

PHOEBE. I changed my mind. Tell the whole story. Tell the whole story with all the details.

SEBASTIAN. You sure? You got real upset last time I told the whole story.

PHOEBE. I'm too stoned to get real upset. Sides it makes you sound like more of a hero. The long version, I mean.

(Beat.)

SEBASTIAN. Okay... ummm... It was cloudy so there was barely anyone at the beach. In fact we were going to go to Atlantic City instead but Ronnie really wanted to swim and it wasn't raining so we drove to Sea Isle. We stopped at that liquor store off the Parkway with that guy who looked like he was in ZZ Top. And when we got to the beach Victor mixed cocktails. For everyone. You drank three gin and tonics out of a blue plastic cup. Victor had one. Ronnie and Jesse had two. And I didn't have any cuz I was hung over from the night before. I was gonna smoke a joint but there was a family only a few feet away and the lifeguard was already staring at us because we were loud and Victor didn't want us to get busted for the alcohol. You skipped to the water. Said you were going to body surf. You swam out. The waves were high because a storm was coming. Victor waded in. He was yelling at you and taking pictures with his digital camera. A big wave came and you swam it out but at the last second you got swept under and we couldn't see you. Jesse and Ronnie were laughing but then Victor yelled "Where is she?" And they stopped. I was on the phone and almost hung up but then you surfaced. Laughing. You were laughing. Stuck your middle finger up towards the horizon. You turned back. Laughing. Then another wave came. But you didn't see this one. It hit you from behind. You disappeared for a second and then came up and went back under. Came up and went back under. The lifeguard was talking to a girl. He didn't see you. Victor went in first. Swam out and grabbed you but you were fighting too hard and pulled him under. Ronnie and Jesse stood up. And then I ran in. Swam and grabbed you from behind pulling you off of Victor. Holding you. The lifeguard was there too by that time. He gave you a paddle board and the four of us swam to shore. I helped you to the blanket while Victor threw up salt water and gin. Ronnie started crying and Jesse held you.

(Beat.)

SEBASTIAN. I don't think yer a fraud. If that's like any consolation.
PHOEBE. You don't know me that well.
SEBASTIAN. True.
PHOEBE. I don't think yer a loser. I mean I used to but I don't now.
SEBASTIAN. Thanks.

(Beat.)

PHOEBE. Can I tell you something?
SEBASTIAN. Sure.
PHOEBE. Its like a secret so... you can't tell anyone... not even Ronnie...
SEBASTIAN. Yeah... sure...
PHOEBE. Whatever my life is...all the sum of it's parts or each part individually... it's like I agreed to them even though I didn't want them and I don't know why... And before I drowned... I was kinda going along with it all... not happy not sad juss- I dunno maybe doin' little things to fuck shit up... but when I drowned... in that moment... fuck- I lost my train of thought...
SEBASTIAN. I think yer ahh little blue friends have kicked in.
PHOEBE. Umm... yeah... fuck...
SEBASTIAN. I get what yer sayin' though... I think...
PHOEBE. Thanks.

(Beat.)

SEBASTIAN. Maybe I should tell you the story again.
PHOEBE. Yeah... yeah tell me the story again...
SEBASTIAN. Do you want to hear long or the short version?
PHOEBE. Ummm... the short version.
SEBASTIAN. Okay.
PHOEBE. Thank you.
SEBASTIAN. We were at the Jersey shore. You swam out. A big wave came. You got pulled under and swept out-

SEBASTIAN. Fuck it. I don't have any place else to be.
PHOEBE. Works for me.

(Beat. He stares at her.)

SEBASTIAN. Ummm... Sheryl dumped me.
PHOEBE. Yeah Ronnie told me. You bummed?
SEBASTIAN. I guess I should be more upset than I actually am.
PHOEBE. I feel the same way about Jesse this morning.
SEBASTIAN. You guys-?
PHOEBE. No, no. I mean when he busted me snorting... I thought I would be humiliated.
SEBASTIAN. And?
PHOEBE. I didn't feel anything.
SEBASTIAN. It's probably the pills.
PHOEBE. Nope don't think so.

(Beat.)

SEBASTIAN. Same way with Sheryl...
PHOEBE. Really?
SEBASTIAN. Yup... you know I was kinda just waiting for the other ball or shoe or whatever the fuck it is to drop anyway...
PHOEBE. Whattaya mean?
SEBASTIAN. I dunno... Sheryl like has motivation...she's gonna be something someday... all that going for your goals crap really isn't my strong suit...
PHOEBE. Well in that respect we're not that different...
SEBASTIAN. Yeah but yer married... you've like put at least a foot into the land of the grown-ups.
PHOEBE. Sure...

(Beat.)

PHOEBE. Do you ever feel like yer a fraud?
SEBASTIAN. A loser yes... a fraud not so much. Why?
PHOEBE. Juss some shit I been thinking about.
SEBASTIAN. Oh.

SEBASTIAN. Look I just wanted to help. You seem like yer in trouble.

(Beat.)

PHOEBE. I'm- I'm not "in trouble".
SEBASTIAN. Really?
PHOEBE. Yes. I'm just confused-er- figuring shit out er-
SEBASTIAN. Phoebe yer popping pills and hanging out with me.
PHOEBE. Jesus are you fucking accusing me of having some sort of like problem?
SEBASTIAN. In my observation problem-free people don't crush those fuckers up and snort them while hiding out from the world.
PHOEBE. Fuck off. I thought you were- Jesus I guess yer juss as insensitive an judgemental as-
SEBASTIAN. No wait I'm not trying to be judgemental.
PHOEBE. Could've fooled me.
SEBASTIAN. I'm just trying to- Look you've got good stuff in your life even if you don't like it so much right now...and if you don't like yer situation don't try to look for a quick way out where there isn't one...

(Beat. PHOEBE gets up. Lights up on MALLORY in JESSE'S office.)

PHOEBE. Sure. I ummm...should go.
SEBASTIAN. You gonna be okay? You should take a cab.
PHOEBE. Yeah.
SEBASTIAN. I'm sorry if I hurt your feelings.
PHOEBE. Yeah. Whatever.
SEBASTIAN. I didn't mean to make you upset. I just-
PHOEBE. Too fuckin' late.
SEBASTIAN. Look this doesn't mean we have to stop meeting and talking about what happened.
PHOEBE. Are you joking?
SEBASTIAN. No I mean it still might help you to get past this-
PHOEBE. I think you've helped enough.

SEBASTIAN. But-
PHOEBE. I'll see ya around.
SEBASTIAN. Phoebe-

(PHOEBE exits.)

SEBASTIAN. Fuck me.

(Lights down on SEBASTIAN. JESSE and MALLORY in JESSE'S office.)

JESSE. Back so soon?
MALLORY. Uhhh... yeah...
JESSE. Change your mind about the trip?
MALLORY. Ummm... sort of... I think...
JESSE. Figures.
MALLORY. What's that supposed to mean?
JESSE. I dunno you just didn't seem the world travelling type.
MALLORY. Oh.
JESSE. Sorry, that came out a little meaner than I intended.
MALLORY. I'm used to it.
JESSE. I have a lot going on.... I mean outside of work.
MALLORY. S'okay.

(Beat.)

JESSE. So did you want to change your departure date? Or change to a round trip?
MALLORY. I'm not sure...
JESSE. You can take a day to think about it. It won't be that much more expensive. Unfortunately though the ticket's non-refundable.
MALLORY. I know.
JESSE. So?

(Beat.)

MALLORY. Ummm can I ask you a personal question?
JESSE. Uhhh... sure... about what?

MALLORY. Your wife.

JESSE. Phoebe?

MALLORY. Yeah I guess.

JESSE. What about her?

MALLORY. When you met her did you know? Did you know you wanted to be with her forever?

JESSE. I guess so... we were really young...

MALLORY. But when you met her...did you have this thing... almost like what they say about dying... where your life flashes before your eyes... but it's not your past it's your future... but with that person...

JESSE. I... I mean I've been with her so long...maybe...

MALLORY. Oh...

JESSE. Sorry.

MALLORY. No, no problem.

(Beat.)

JESSE. Somebody make you change your mind about the trip?

MALLORY. No... Maybe... I'm not sure.

JESSE. It happens to the best of us.

MALLORY. You too?

JESSE. I guess... you know but she gave up stuff too. You have to, to be in a relationship.

MALLORY. Was it worth it?

(Pause.)

JESSE. You should go on the trip.

(Lights down on JESSE and MALLORY. Lights up on RONNIE and VICTOR on the subway.)

VICTOR... So after fucking around in the park a little bit I ran into you.

RONNIE. Shit. That's what I would call a day.

VICTOR. I know.

RONNIE. Wow, sitting here right now. You totally betray the rules of the shoe game.

VICTOR. The what?
RONNIE. The shoe game.
VICTOR. I don't get it.
RONNIE. Okay, look at that guy's shoes.
VICTOR. Who?
RONNIE. The dude wearing a business suit with clogs. What is that all about?
VICTOR. Comfort.
RONNIE. No way Vic, that is clearly a case of a secret life going on.
VICTOR. How do you know?
RONNIE. You can always tell a person's true self by their shoes. Clothes you can fake. But shoes... shoes they always give you away.
VICTOR. So what do beat up Converse say about you?
RONNIE. That I'm fuckin' broke ass.
VICTOR. So my loafers are lying.
RONNIE. Yup. They definitely don't say unemployed.
VICTOR. I was planning on retiring them to the back of my closet anyway.
RONNIE. You can get another teaching job anywhere.
VICTOR. I don't wanna teach anymore.
RONNIE. So what the fuck are you gonna do then?
VICTOR. I dunno.
RONNIE. The bills aren't gonna pay themselves.
VICTOR. I am fully aware of that.
RONNIE. Hey weren't you at some point gonna be the Chester Bangs of the twenty-first century or something?
VICTOR. It's Lester Bangs.
RONNIE. So what about bein' that?
VICTOR. Look I just freed myself from the shackles of public education. I kinda juss feel like seein' where the day takes me.
RONNIE. Well you could always be a jolly green grocer like me and Phebes. But then again I dunno if you could handle the glamour of it all.
VICTOR. No thanks. By the way are you crashing at my place tonight?
RONNIE. Nope the bitch is gone. She dumped him. Finally.
VICTOR. Good cuz I have a date.
RONNIE. How did you fail to mention that in your big story?

VICTOR. Oh weird. I dunno. It's been a crazy day.

RONNIE. Clearly. Jesus man, you walked out on your job, got drunk and nabbed a date all in one day?

VICTOR. Yup.

RONNIE. Shit I should be taking lessons from you. Maybe then I wouldn't be living in a world of pain with Sebastian.

VICTOR. I did something drastic about my situation and feel better than I have in two years.

RONNIE. True. But I don't hate Sebastian.

VICTOR. Oh we all know that. We all know that because it consumes your life and at least a third of every conversation you have.

RONNIE. Come on. It does not.

VICTOR. You're like the Jersey version of Morrissey.

RONNIE. Gimme a break. I gotta give him time. I don't wanna be the rebound girl.

VICTOR. You have an excuse for everything.

RONNIE. We all have to be good at something.

VICTOR. Why are you attracted to him anyway? He's a bump on a log if you ask me.

RONNIE I'm a sucker for a fixer upper. So sue me.

VICTOR I think yer just a sucker.

RONNIE. So then what's with the encouragement?

VICTOR. Because regardless of how I feel you still need to tell him how you feel. Because I would like you to finally fucking shut up about him.

RONNIE. Whatever.

(She rolls her eyes at him. Beat.)

RONNIE. Hey, has Phoebe been calling you lately?
VICTOR. Not more than usual.
RONNIE. I thought so...
VICTOR. Why?
RONNIE. Her and Sebastian have been hanging out.
VICTOR. Here we go again.
RONNIE. Just humor me for a hot minute, okay?
VICTOR. Fine, fine.
RONNIE. So did you know they've been hanging out?
VICTOR. Yeah I guess.

RONNIE. Oh....What do ummm...you think of all that?

VICTOR. I think she's mad at Jesse.

RONNIE. She's always mad at Jesse. They're like the couple who should've broken up senior year of high school like everybody else did.

VICTOR. I guess he takes that till death do us part thing seriously.

RONNIE. Guess I'm not the only sucker we know.

VICTOR. Ha. Ha.

(Beat.)

RONNIE. Soooo... you think maybe something's going on with her and Sebastian?

VICTOR. No.

RONNIE. But she's not calling you.

VICTOR. She's not calling me cuz I would've told her to get over it.

RONNIE. I find that hard to believe.

(Beat.)

VICTOR. See that homeless guy at the other end of the train.

RONNIE. Yeah.

VICTOR. Watch when he comes through. Most of the people won't look at him.

RONNIE. Okay...

(They turn their heads and watch as if someone is walking past them on the train.)

RONNIE. So yer point?

VICTOR. They won't look at him not because they don't care but because they care too much.

RONNIE. They're not looking at him because they don't wanna give him money.

VICTOR. That's part of it.

RONNIE. Okay.

VICTOR. Everybody here on the train has their own bullshit in their own lives and some days your own bullshit...it's too bad to take on anybody else's. Ya gotta keep your skin thick sometimes just to make it through the day.

RONNIE. So what's your point?

VICTOR. Sebastian doesn't seem to have much bullshit.

RONNIE. You don't live with him.

VICTOR. He doesn't have much of anything. Or maybe he's not as cold blooded as the rest of us. Whichever way you look at it he'll give the change to the homeless guy.

RONNIE. You're losing me with the metaphor, dude.

VICTOR. He'll look at the homeless guy and give him change. He'll take on somebody else's bullshit. It makes him feel better about himself. That's all it is with him and Phoebe.

RONNIE. You gotta lotta brains in that head of yours.

VICTOR. It's a metaphor I stole from Lester Bangs from this deconstruction of a Van Morrison album he wrote.

RONNIE. And you're over being a rock critic, huh?

VICTOR. I'm living in the moment, remember?

RONNIE. Right, right...

(Beat.)

RONNIE. God, we really should be doing more with our small lives.

VICTOR. I think you have to get your own shit together before you can affect change on the world.

RONNIE. Good way to justify quitting your job...

VICTOR. Or a good way to justify you finally being truthful with Sebastian.

RONNIE. Yeah.

VICTOR. I'm serious.

RONNIE. *(Sarcastically.)* Cuz me and Sebastian getting together will totally bring about world peace.

VICTOR. Everybody's shits gotta start somewhere.

RONNIE. Hey my dream may be small but it's still my dream.

VICTOR. If it's small it shouldn't be that hard to attain right?

RONNIE. Riiight...this is my stop dude. Lemme know how your date goes.

(Lights down on VICTOR and RONNIE. Lights up on JESSE on the stoop of an apartment building in Queens. He paces. MALLORY exits the building and comes down the stairs.)

JESSE. Hey.
MALLORY. Oh... hey...
JESSE. I got your address from your ticket booking.
MALLORY. Oh... umm what are you doing here?
JESSE. I ummm... I'm not sure...
MALLORY. Oh.

(Beat.)

MALLORY. I hafta meet someone-
JESSE. I juss-I juss need to talk to you for a minute.
MALLORY. About my trip?
JESSE. Not really.
MALLORY. Oh.
JESSE. Look what you said in the office it made me think about shit.
MALLORY. Oh.
JESSE. I wasn't totally honest with you.
MALLORY. About what?
JESSE. Phoebe...my wife...
MALLORY. Oh that's okay.
JESSE. No it's not.
MALLORY. It's not?
JESSE. Just hear me out okay. I really just need somebody to hear me out.
MALLORY. Umm...sure.
JESSE. Look I did feel that way about her... that way you said... I felt that way about her and it never went away and it was so fuckin' bad I gave up alotta shit to be with her...
MALLORY. So I uhhh...shouldn't go on my trip?
JESSE. No. I dunno...
MALLORY. I'm confused.
JESSE. It's just that see the feeling... it's not a guarantee... I gave up all this shit to be with her and now I work a crappy job at a travel agency because she's spending our money on pills er god knows what... and she won't look at me... and what we had before...
MALLORY. It's disappeared?
JESSE. No. Yes. Not exactly.
MALLORY. I don't understand.

JESSE. She's disappeared...not literally... I mean she's still at home... a human being sitting there... but she's gone... the Phoebe I knew is gone... inside I guess... I mean I look at her.... into her fuckin' eyes and there's nothing there... I mean there's something there but nothing I recognize...and I keep thinking about our honeymoon... not in some sad, romantic things were blissful kind of way... but in this- see we went to Scotland and took this boat tour of Lochness... ya know that place where the monster supposedly is... and anyway she wandered to the other end of the boat and this guy started telling me... just me mind you...that the monster isn't a monster it's actually these reptiles that live at the bottom of the lake... and the lake is really dense... so dense that you can't see the bottom... and that these reptiles that live in the lake they swim around all happy and shit but when they lose their way that's when they come to the surface... to orient themselves... thats when we see them ya know... when they're lost... anyway I guess I just keep hoping that happens with Phoebe, cuz she's lost... and I can't seem to find her in there... in all that denseness beneath her eyes... and I hope whatever it is comes to the surface... I just want her to come to the surface....

MALLORY. Wow... I'm sorry...

JESSE. So I guess just do what you have to do for yourself cuz... this guy... I don't know what your situation is-

MALLORY. He's the first person to ever tell me I was pretty-

JESSE. Yeah well it doesn't always work out the way-

MALLORY. No he's the first person in my entire life.

JESSE. Oh.

(Beat.)

MALLORY. If we had had this conversation years ago before things got bad what would you have told me to do?

JESSE. Stay.

MALLORY. Huh...

JESSE. But I know better now.

MALLORY. Look, I have to see what happens at least for today.

JESSE. The ticket's non-refundable.

MALLORY. I know.

(Beat.)

MALLORY. Why do you care so much?
JESSE. I guess I just wished someone would've said this to me.
MALLORY. Maybe ummm...maybe they did and ummm you didn't listen.

(Beat.)

MALLORY. I should get going. I don't wanna be late.
JESSE. Yeah...
MALLORY. I'll let you know about the ticket...
JESSE. Sure...
MALLORY. I'm sorry about your wife.
JESSE. Yeah, me too.

(She exits. JESSE is alone. Lights down. Lights up on SEBASTIAN on his cell phone. He dials a number.)

SEBASTIAN. Hey Sheryl... its me Sebastian... I know... I know you told me not to call you... which is probably why you're not picking up... or maybe you're not home... but I'd like to think that you are there sitting on your pink couch listening to this- Dammit.

(He re-dials the number.)

SEBASTIAN. Hey it's me again... I think your answering machine cut me off or something... anyway... I thought about what you said... and I'll admit that it appears like I don't have much motivation in life... I do ummm... play a lot of video games... and you're right I guess um... a Philosophy degree isn't really gonna get me anywhere... but I just wanna tell you- Fuck!

(He dials the number again.)

SEBASTIAN. Me again... I think you're answering machine is fucked- anyway what I want you to know is that I saved this girl at the beach a few months ago... She was drowning and I swam out and I saved her... I don't even really like her that much and I swam out and I saved her... I coulda just sat on the beach like everybody else... and she keeps telling me she owes me her life... and she needs me Sheryl... this girl for whatever reason... she needs me in her life... somebody needs me and she can see I'm not a loser... so all of this... all of this you should know because it proves... it proves I do, do shit... I'm not just a waste of space... and I just want you to think about that because I don't think Phil the party promoter or whatever his fucking name is woulda done something like I did... cool... ummm call me back... Bye...

(Lights out on SEBASTIAN. Lights up on MALLORY and VICTOR at the bar The Other Room in the West Village.)

MALLORY. It's really dark in here.
VICTOR. Yeah, I like to think of it as cozy.

(Beat.)

VICTOR. They play Tapes n' Tapes and Snow Patrol and Radiohead. On a rare night they'll actually play the Velvet Underground.
MALLORY. Oh.
VICTOR. You into that kind of music?
MALLORY. I don't really know umm much about that kind of music.
VICTOR. Oh.
MALLORY. But I'm sure it's great.
VICTOR. Yeah I think you'd like it...

(Beat.)

VICTOR. We can go some place else if you want.
MALLORY. No,no I like it. It's cozy like you said.

(Beat.)

VICTOR. So...
MALLORY. Yeah.

(Beat.)

VICTOR. I'm sorry about earlier today.
MALLORY. Why?
VICTOR. I'm actually very normal. That whole- well when we met- I was just- I don't act like that all the time.
MALLORY. You were endearing.
VICTOR. I was?
MALLORY. In a manic sort of way.
VICTOR. Yeah, I guess so.

(Beat.)

VICTOR. I was surprised you said yes.
MALLORY. Me too.

(Beat.)

MALLORY. But I'm- I'm glad I'm here now.
VICTOR. Me too.

(Beat.)

VICTOR. The candlelight-
MALLORY. What?
VICTOR. The candlelight... it's pretty the way it reflects off your glasses.
MALLORY. Oh. Umm... that's a nice shirt.
VICTOR. Thanks.

(Beat.)

MALLORY. So ummm did you always want to be a teacher?
VICTOR. No...nope. I wanted to be a rock critic.
MALLORY. Like a geologist?
VICTOR. No, no like rock music. I wanted to be the next great rock critic.
MALLORY. Oh. Sorry. I'm not that into pop culture.
VICTOR. That's okay.
MALLORY. So what happened?

VICTOR. Went to a lot of shows. Had a lot of well-thought, eloquent opinions but only a few reviews in the Brooklyn Rail. Never really got further than that. So I became a teacher. Steadier than working at a coffee shop tryin' to be somethin that's not happenin'.

(Beat.)

MALLORY. I dunno maybe you weren't supposed to be a teacher.
VICTOR. Whattaya mean?
MALLORY. I like to believe that if you really want something bad enough you'll figure out a way to make it happen.
VICTOR. Yeah... well... um... at twenty-eight I think I'm a little old to be breaking into the music business.
MALLORY. Well maybe then it's time for a new dream.
VICTOR. Huh?
MALLORY. Just because you had to give up an old dream doesn't mean you can't have a new one.
VICTOR. Wow... yeah... I never thought of it that way.
MALLORY. Sorry. That sorta all juss came out-
VICTOR. No. Thank you.

(Beat.)

VICTOR. Anyway enough about me. So ummm where do you work what do you do?
MALLORY. Oh umm... well I was a book keeper at a law firm... up until a week ago...
VICTOR. A book keeper wow...
MALLORY. I'm good with numbers.
VICTOR. I'm bet you're good at alotta stuff.

(Beat.)

VICTOR. God... sorry sometimes things come out the wrong way-
MALLORY. No, no it's fine.
VICTOR. I suck at flirting.

MALLORY. I'm not much better.
VICTOR. I'm not skeevy, really.
MALLORY. I know I wouldn't be here if you were.

(Beat.)

MALLORY. Sorry...
VICTOR. For what?
MALLORY. I don't go out much...
VICTOR. On dates? Me neither really.
MALLORY. No I meant in general.
VICTOR. Oh.
MALLORY. This umm is actually my first time-
VICTOR. Out at a bar?
MALLORY. No ummm... on a date.
VICTOR. Really?
MALLORY. Yeah.
VICTOR. If it makes you feel any better I've only had a string of bad ones.
MALLORY. Bad what?
VICTOR. Dates.
MALLORY. Oh.
VICTOR. But you, you're doing a good job. I mean a good job on this date.
MALLORY. Thanks. You too.

(Beat.)

MALLORY. I uhhh... I have a fish. And I knit. And I live in Brooklyn.
VICTOR. Huh?
MALLORY. You ummm asked me about myself...
VICTOR. Right, right... And you told me you're going on a trip.
MALLORY. Right... yeah... I'm ahhh... I'm going on a trip.
VICTOR. You don't sound so sure of that anymore.

(Beat.)

VICTOR. Sorry, is it a sore subject?

MALLORY. I booked a trip to Brazil. A one way trip to Brazil. I've saved twenty thousand dollars to go there.
VICTOR. Oh.
MALLORY. Yeah...
VICTOR. Usually girls tell me at the end of the date that we're not going out again.
MALLORY. No it's not you... I mean I had booked the trip before-
VICTOR. I know I was just kidding.
MALLORY. Oh.
VICTOR. I guess ummm I just meant to say you're really nice and it sucks we won't get to hang out again.
MALLORY. Yeah...

(Beat.)

MALLORY. Can I be honest with you?
VICTOR. Sure... were you not being honest before?
MALLORY. I was... I mean I am all those things I said before-
VICTOR. Oh good cuz that would be weird on a first date to lie - although I've had that happen before.
MALLORY. I just sort of didn't tell you everything.
VICTOR. You're not a lesbian are you? Cuz I've had that happen before to.
MALLORY. No, no... totally straight.
VICTOR. Whew... okay explain away then.
MALLORY. Ummm... see... My sister and I... I have a sister... she's older she's a lawyer now but anyway...when we were younger we got these dolls... they were these dolls that supposedly you ordered them to look like you... then you and your doll are like twins... it's supposed to be fun... so they arrived and Leslie, my sister opened her doll first and it looked just like her, ya know... long blond hair... big blue eyes... and this perfect little button nose... and then I opened my doll... and... it was perfect looking just like hers... but it didn't look like me... there were no glasses... or mousey brown hair... or crooked teeth...
VICTOR. You're moving to Brazil because of a doll?
MALLORY. No. Well sort of...
VICTOR. I don't get it.

MALLORY. See it's been like that forever ya know... like that moment with the doll... cuz I wasn't one of those un-pretty girls who cultivated some sort of alternative funny personality... I've never been risky or slutty or even that personable... and then in high school this girl in my math class got a nose job... she was one of those girls who wasn't that pretty but wasn't un-pretty she was just sort of there... but after the nose job... she was different or everyone around her treated her differently... whatever it doesn't matter... she was happier... so I started saving... worked all through high school... two jobs in community college... did tons of research and when I had saved enough I booked the trip to Brazil... because they have the best most affordable plastic surgery...

VICTOR. Wow...

MALLORY. I wanted to make a change... a big change... I wanted to take a big risk...become somebody else... because this... I was tired of being this...

VICTOR. Jesus Christ...

MALLORY. But then you asked me on a date...

VICTOR. I did.

MALLORY. No one's really ever looked at me... or talked to me out of the blue for that matter... I mean sometimes I feel like I just blend in... with the surroundings... but you...

(Beat.)

MALLORY. I'm sorry maybe I shouldn't have been so honest...

(Beat.)

MALLORY. Please say something...

VICTOR. I think you're very brave...

MALLORY. But?

VICTOR. No buts... an "and" maybe...

MALLORY. And?

VICTOR. And I think it's really beautiful that you felt like you could be that open with me.

MALLORY. Oh... good...

(Beat.)

>VICTOR. I wanna show you something...
>MALLORY. Okay...
>VICTOR. It's in the Bronx. Do you mind taking the train?

(Lights out on VICTOR and MALLORY. Lights up on JESSE and PHOEBE at home.)

>PHOEBE. There's nothing in the fridge you probably wanna order something if you're hungry.
>JESSE. We don't have enough money to order something.
>PHOEBE. Well I ate.
>JESSE. I'll just gnaw on the kitchen table or something I guess.
>PHOEBE. Don't be passive aggressive.
>JESSE. What do you want me to be then Phoebe?
>PHOEBE. I dunno make a choice for yourself for once.
>JESSE. I've made plenty of choices for myself.
>PHOEBE. *(Mumbling.)* Not the right ones if you ask me.
>JESSE. What?
>PHOEBE. Nothing.
>JESSE. Maybe I should make choices like you Phoebe and work at a grocery store and spend my time taking pills instead of looking for a real job.
>PHOEBE. My job is a real job.
>JESSE., For people like Ronnie who don't have aspirations beyond being mediocre.
>PHOEBE. Umm excuse me but you work at a fucking travel agency Jesse.
>JESSE. Because you seem to be putting what little money we have up your nose.
>PHOEBE. That's low.
>JESSE. It's true.
>PHOEBE. Fuck you.

(Beat.)

>JESSE. What am I supposed to do Phoebe?
>PHOEBE. I dunno yer a grown-up decide for yourself.

JESSE. And be completely selfish like you?

PHOEBE. What's that supposed to mean?

JESSE. Every decision I've made since we got here have been decisions for us- for you... to make you happy.

PHOEBE. Don't be the martyr.

JESSE. I gave up Cornell and went to a state college to be with you.

PHOEBE. I didn't force you Jesse.

JESSE. I moved to New York City because that's what made you happy. And even though we agreed that you would get a job at a museum so I could write, I got that shitty job when the best thing you could come up with was bagging groceries.

PHOEBE. Are you done?

JESSE. No. I have stood by you through this whole drowning thing and and nothing I do seems to be working Phebes. Cuz all you seem to be doing is taking more and more pills.

PHOEBE. The doctor prescribed those to me.

JESSE. For a week. I looked at the original bottle. He gave you a weeks prescription.

PHOEBE. And then he gave me another one.

JESSE. For three months? He gave you a three month prescription for Valium?

PHOEBE. You don't go with me to the doctor you have no idea what you're talking about.

JESSE. You haven't been to the doctor in the last two months.

PHOEBE. You don't know what I do when you're not around.

JESSE. Really? Cuz my guess is you're buying that stuff from someone else and fucking snorting it. Fucking crushing it up and snorting it. And not even in secret. You fucking snort it in front of me. What do you wanna get caught?

(Pause. She looks away from him.)

JESSE. You have nothing to say?

(Beat.)

PHOEBE. I don't want this anymore.

JESSE. I don't want this anymore either. I wanna be back to the way we were before.

PHOEBE. No. You didn't save me when I was drowning.

JESSE. What are you talking about?

PHOEBE. You were supposed to save me at the beach and you didn't. Sebastian did.

JESSE. Wait. Is that what this is all about?

PHOEBE. Maybe.

JESSE. Fuck you Phoebe. You can't put all the bad shit between us on one moment.

PHOEBE. Well don't you think that one moment is pretty enlightening about the state of our relationship?

JESSE. You think I wanted you to drown?

PHOEBE. No I'm- I guess I'm just starting to realize that things happen for a reason... to show you that certain stuff in your life is working or not working.

JESSE. What are you talking about?

PHOEBE. I wanted to go to college by myself. I wanted to come to New York by myself. I wanted to be able to make the decision whether or not I wanted to work in a fucking museum or a grocery store or whatever by myself.

JESSE. Don't sit here and tell me that you got sucked into the undertow and suddenly resurfaced and decided yer life is shit cuz I didn't save you. That doesn't happen Phoebe it just doesn't.

PHOEBE. Well it did-

JESSE. Cuz this sorta shit isn't something you just have an epiphany about one day. This is the sorta shit you like feel the whole time you're going through life and you tuck away till it's built up.

(Beat.)

JESSE. Have you been feeling this the whole time?

(Beat.)

PHOEBE. I think I didn't want any of this to begin with.

JESSE. So while I've been in love with you this whole time. While I've given up everything for you, you've been just building up resentment?

PHOEBE. Don't make it like that Jesse. God, you're so much more in love with playing the martyr than you are with me.

JESSE. How dare you fucking say that.

PHOEBE. Jesse don't you see? You would have jumped in. You would have jumped in if deep down inside you didn't feel the same way too.

JESSE. I'm sorry. I'm sorry I didn't jump in.

PHOEBE. Jesse this isn't working.

JESSE. Well what the fuck are we supposed to do now?

PHOEBE. I don't think there is a we...

JESSE. We're married. There is a we.

(Beat.)

JESSE. Phoebe?

PHOEBE. I don't think I want to be with you anymore.

JESSE. You don't think, or you know...

(Beat.)

PHOEBE. I know.

JESSE. What?

PHOEBE. Don't make me say it again.

JESSE. Jesus Christ Phoebe we've been together for almost ten years. You can't just fucking end it like this. There has to be like some way we can work through it.

PHOEBE. No... there isn't.

JESSE. We could get you off the pills. We could go to couple's therapy-

PHOEBE. No Jesse! No! I don't want to fucking be with you anymore okay? And deep down inside whether you admit it or not you don't want to be with me either.

JESSE. I do wanna be with you. I just wish you would be the person I used to know.

PHOEBE. But I'm not. And I don't ever really think I was that person. And nothing you do or say is gonna make any of this better!

JESSE. Well what the hell am I supposed to do now?

PHOEBE. I dunno what you're supposed to do now. Maybe fucking do something for yourself instead of trying to change me.

(Beat.)

JESSE. Get out. I don't wanna fucking look at you.
PHOEBE. What?
JESSE. You want me to make a fucking decision for myself that doesn't take you into consideration then I'm making one right now. Get out.
PHOEBE. Where am I supposed to go?
JESSE. Try swimming. You seem to have luck figuring your life out there.

(PHOEBE exits. Lights dim on JESSE. Later that night. Lights up on MALLORY and VICTOR they stand in streetlight over a tiny gravestone made of popsicle sticks.)

MALLORY. It's beautiful.
VICTOR. It's just some popsicle sticks...
MALLORY. No but the gesture... is... most people wouldn't do that...
VICTOR. Yeah I guess not...
MALLORY. You must've been a good teacher.
VICTOR. Some days...
MALLORY. You sad you're not one anymore?
VICTOR. Right now, no. Tomorrow, maybe...
MALLORY. Oh.
VICTOR. Look, I just really wanna be here right now with you...and just have that be the only thing I'm doing...and tomorrow I'll think about tomorrow...
MALLORY. Sounds good.

(Beat.)

MALLORY. We should say a prayer or something. Don't people usually do that at gravesites?
VICTOR. Sure.

(Beat.)

MALLORY. I don't know any prayers do you?

VICTOR. Ummm... No...

(Beat.)

VICTOR. Maybe we could just hold hands and have a moment of silence instead.
MALLORY. Okay.

(They hold hands. On the opposite side of the stage RONNIE enters the living room of her apartment. SEBASTIAN is asleep sprawled out on a bean bag chair. A Play Station control, is dangling from his hands. A few beer bottles are scattered around him. She sits down in the other beanbag chair. She pokes SEBASTIAN a few times.)

RONNIE. Sebastian.

(Beat. She pokes again.)

RONNIE. Sebastian.
SEBASTIAN. Huh?
RONNIE. You hang with Phoebe?
SEBASTIAN. What? Yeah...
RONNIE. She okay?

(VICTOR and MALLORY end their moment of silence. They look at each other.)

SEBASTIAN. I unno... Ron I'm tired...
MALLORY. What?
VICTOR. You're beautiful...
RONNIE. Sebastian?

(SEBASTIAN is half asleep. VICTOR grabs MALLORY and kisses her.)

SEBASTIAN. Hmm?
RONNIE. I love you.
SEBASTIAN. Mmmm... you too.

(MALLORY throws her arms around VICTOR.)

    RONNIE. No I'm in love with you.
    SEBASTIAN. *(Almost asleep.)* Whah?
    RONNIE. Nothing.

(MALLORY and VICTOR keep kissing. SEBASTIAN snores. Blue light up on PHOEBE. She is near water and looks at it tentatively.)

    RONNIE. I'm in love with you Sebastian. I'm in love with you.

(SEBASTIAN does not stir. PHOEBE stands at the edge. She strips down to her underwear, closes her eyes and puts her hands up as if to dive in. Lights out.)

End of play

**Also by
Megan Mostyn-Brown...**

girl.

**The Secret Lives
of Losers**

Please visit our website **samuelfrench.com** for complete
descriptions and licensing information.